THE UNITED STATES
REGION BY REGION

Written by Patricia K. Kummer

STECK-VAUGHN

A Harcourt Company

www.steck-vaughn.com

Contents

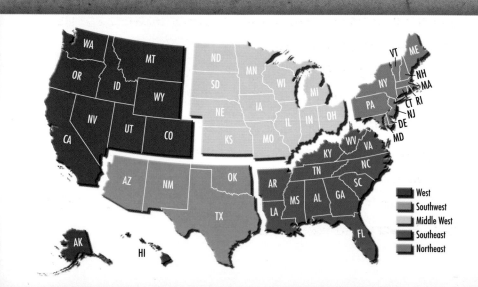

INTRODUCTION

From the Atlantic Ocean to the Pacific, from Canada to Mexico, the United States covers almost 4 million square miles (6 million square kilometers). It's a big country. To understand it, we look at it in different ways. Sometimes we look at it as one country whose capital is Washington, D.C. At other times we think about each of its fifty states. We also look at its five **regions.** A region is an area of land with at least one feature that sets it apart from other areas. Features that make an area a region include its landforms (such as mountains and plains) and its **climate.** Other regional features are an area's history and the way its people make a living.

Each United States region is known for at least one special feature. The Northeast has large cities. The Southeast is famous for cotton, peanuts, and other crops that grow in its warm climate. The Middle West has millions of acres of farmland. The Southwest is known for its deserts and unusual landforms. The West has **glaciers** and tall mountains.

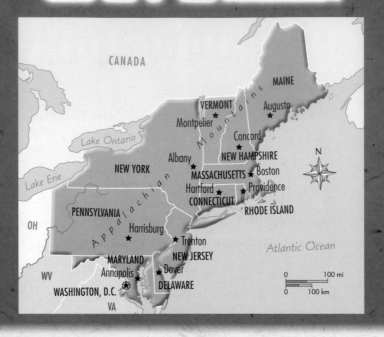

The Northeast contains 11 states and is the smallest region of the United States, but it has some important features that set it apart from others. Some of the largest United States cities lie in the Northeast. Many of these cities sit in large protected **harbors** carved by the Atlantic Ocean. Farther **inland,** the northern peaks of the Appalachian Mountains rise from the land.

Before the United States became a country, people from Great Britain came to live in the Northeast. In the years that followed, the people of the Northeast played an important part in the birth of a new nation.

Boston, Massachusetts; New York, New York; Philadelphia, Pennsylvania; Baltimore, Maryland; and Washington, D.C., are some of the country's biggest cities. In fact, New York City is the largest city in the United States. About 40 million people live in the area from Boston to Washington, D.C. This long strip of end-to-end cities is called a **megalopolis.**

Northeasterners enjoy many activities in their big cities. People can find something fun to do at almost any hour in New York City. That's why New York City is called "the City That Never Sleeps." Some New York City restaurants stay open all night. During the day bikers, runners, roller skaters, and horseback riders use paths in Central Park. Other people visit New York's world-famous art museums. At night the bright lights of Broadway draw people to plays and concerts.

New York City lights at night

The capital of the United States, Washington, D.C., lies in the Northeast region, but it is not a state or even part of a state. This city is known as a district—an area set up for a special purpose. *D.C.* stands for "District of Columbia." Washington, D.C., became the nation's capital in 1800. The Capitol building stands at one end of the National Mall, a long, grassy rectangular park. The Lincoln Memorial stands at the opposite end of the Mall. In the middle of the Mall, the Washington Monument points skyward. It is the capital city's tallest building.

All sorts of museums line the Mall, and many of them are part of the Smithsonian Institution. The Smithsonian's National Air and Space Museum has the Wright Brothers' first airplane and the first spaceship that landed on the moon. The National Museum of History has a set of George Washington's false teeth.

The Northeast region has played an important part in United States history. Nine of the original 13 British colonies were in the Northeast. When the colonies broke away from Great Britain's rule, they fought in the Revolutionary War (1775–1783). The first battle of the

The Liberty Bell in Philadelphia

war took place in Lexington, Massachusetts. Footprints painted on some sidewalks in Boston mark the Freedom Trail, a group of places that were important during the Revolutionary War. The Declaration of Independence was signed in Philadelphia, Pennsylvania, and the United States Constitution was written there.

During the Civil War (1861–1865), all the states in the Northeast region belonged to what was called the Union. Several southern states had left the Union. They set up a new government called the Confederate States of America. As part of the Union Army, soldiers from the Northeast fought to bring the southern states back into the Union. They helped to make the United States a united country again.

An important battle of the Civil War took place at Gettysburg, Pennsylvania.

Another of the Northeast region's features is the Atlantic Ocean. The Atlantic has always been important to people in the Northeast. Since the 1600s, many people have made their living from fishing, whaling, and shipbuilding.

Northeastern fishers are famous for their shellfish catches. Fishers in Maine catch more lobsters than fishers in any other state. Lobsters seem to like Maine's cold Atlantic waters. Maryland is known for crab fishing, and its clam catch beats Maine's. People from

The rocky coast of Maine

Rhode Island call their clams quahogs (KWOH hahgz), a name that comes from American Indians.

Besides catching shellfish, Northeasterners like to eat shellfish. Some Northeasterners are famous for their clambakes. First they dig a deep hole on the beach. Then they line the hole with rocks, build a fire, and place more rocks on the fire. Once the rocks are hot enough, they bake clams, crabs, mussels, and other shellfish on the hot rocks. In Maryland, crabs are a favorite food, and there are many festivals that center around crabs. People have fun cracking open the crab shells with small wooden hammers.

From the 1600s through the middle 1800s, whaling was an important business in the Northeast region. Crews on wooden whaling ships caught whales and removed the oil from whale blubber. The oil was burned in lanterns and used to make candles. At Mystic Seaport in Mystic, Connecticut, people can learn about life on a whaling ship from the 1800s. Mystic was once the country's busiest whaling village. Today whales continue to make money for the Northeast region. Tourists can go out on special boats and watch for humpback and finback whales.

Some Northeasterners still make their living by building ships. People on the Narragansett (nayr uh GAN suht) Bay in Rhode Island build sailboats, motor boats, and yachts (yahtz).

Another feature of the Northeast is the northern part of the Appalachian Mountains. This system of mountains runs from Maine to Alabama. New Hampshire's Mount Washington is the Northcast's highest point. It is part of the Appalachian Mountain system. The highest wind speed ever recorded any place on Earth was at Mount Washington. In 1934 the wind speed was measured at 231 miles (372 kilometers) an hour!

From the Appalachians come the Northeast's important minerals. Huge amounts of **granite** and **marble** can be found in these mountains. Both are used to make such things as buildings, statues, and monuments.

The Appalachians also provide Northeasterners with fun and ways to relax. Skiers speed down slopes in Vermont. More people climb New Hampshire's Mount Monadnock than any other mountain in North America. Other people hike along the Appalachian National Scenic Trail.

A New England town

Within the Northeast region lies New England. This region-within-a-region includes the states of Maine, Vermont, New Hampshire, Connecticut, Massachusetts, and Rhode Island. New England got its name from colonists who came there from England in the 1600s. Today, as in colonial times, New England is known for its small towns. A large grassy area called a village green sits in the middle of many New England towns. Shops, homes, a school, and the town hall can still be found around many village greens.

Most of the Southeast region lies along the Atlantic Ocean and the Gulf of Mexico. Unlike the Northeast, the Southeast has wide, sandy shores. Away from the shore, gently rolling land covers most of the Southeast's 12 states. A warm, wet climate allows cotton and many other kinds of plants to grow on the Southeast's rich land. The Southeast also contains the southern part of the Appalachian Mountains. Unlike the Appalachians in the Northeast, those in the Southeast are known for their coal and dense forests. These natural resources help bring **industries** to the Southeast.

Florida's Miami Beach

Huge sandy beaches line the Southeast's Atlantic and Gulf coasts. Southeasterners who live in Florida are lucky because no matter where they live, they are no more than a two-hour drive from a beach. That's because Florida is a **peninsula** with beaches on both the Atlantic Ocean and the Gulf of Mexico. People in Virginia Beach, Virginia, can walk for 28 miles (46 kilometers) along the longest stretch of beach in the United States. At Myrtle Beach, South Carolina, 10,000 people built the world's longest sand sculpture in 1991. This sand sculpture was as long as 288 football fields!

Sometimes Southeasterners on the coasts have to run for cover when a hurricane blows in. This kind of storm brings high winds, heavy rain, and much destruction.

13

In 1969 Hurricane Camille hit the states of Mississippi and Louisiana. It caused injury and destruction and split an island in two! In 1996 Hurricane Fran blasted Virginia and North Carolina, causing incredible damage. Fran's wind and water brought damage all the way into West Virginia.

The Southeast has warm temperatures and plenty of rainfall. This kind of climate and the Southeast's rich soil help farmers to grow a wide variety of crops. The crop that grows across most of the Southeast is cotton. Mississippi leads the Southeastern states with about 2 million bales of cotton a year. Each bale weighs 480 pounds (218 kilograms). That's the weight of about seven fourth graders!

For many years in the early 1900s, an insect called the boll weevil (bohl WEE vuhl) destroyed cotton

Farmers and machines at work in a cotton field

crops. Southeastern farmers learned that they shouldn't depend only on cotton. They started planting peanuts, sweet potatoes, and other crops. The people of Enterprise, Alabama, wanted to remember the lesson they learned from the boll weevil. They built the Boll Weevil Monument. It is the only United States monument that honors an insect.

The Southeast's warm, wet climate also helps kudzu grow. Kudzu is a fast-growing vine that came from Japan. People brought it to the Southeast to grow as food for cows and goats. The United States government also had people plant kudzu to keep soil from washing away. Today Southeasterners consider kudzu to be a weed that grows out of control. Kudzu covers almost 11,000 square miles (18,000 square kilometers) of the Southeast region.

A vine may not seem like a serious problem, but kudzu is. Kudzu grows so fast that it can cover anything it comes in contact with—trees, bushes, power lines, and even buildings. Some scientists are working on a way to control the growth of kudzu. In the meantime, some Southeasterners use kudzu vines to make baskets. Others make jellies and syrups from the plant.

Spanish moss hangs from the trees around this old home in Louisiana.

Spanish moss is another plant that grows only in the Southeast. This plant doesn't have roots. It drapes itself in the branches of trees and gets water from the air.

Besides beaches, farmland, and unusual plants, the Southeast also has the southern end of the Appalachian Mountains. The Blue Ridge Mountains are part of the southern Appalachian Mountains. These mountains were named for the blue color they have when viewed from a distance.

The Great Smoky Mountains are also in the southern Appalachians. These mountains are named for the smoky-looking mist that hangs over them. Great Smoky Mountains National Park is the most-visited national park in the United States. More than 10 million people go there every year.

People in the Southeast love their Blue Ridge and Smoky mountains. Many songs have been written about them. "The Trail of the Lonesome Pine" tells of the Blue Ridge Mountains, and "On Top of Old Smoky" is about the Smoky Mountains.

West Virginia is known as the Mountain State. The Allegheny, Blue Ridge, and other Appalachian Mountain ranges cover this state. Some people have said that if West Virginia's mountains were smoothed out, the state would cover the rest of the United States, except Alaska and Hawaii.

The Great Smoky Mountains

Valuable minerals lie in the Southeast's Appalachian Mountains. This region is known for its coal, iron, and **limestone.** These three minerals are needed to produce steel. By using these minerals, workers in Birmingham, Alabama, can make much of the country's steel.

Besides minerals, the Southeast also has many underground caves. Mammoth Cave in Kentucky is the longest cave in the world. It winds for more than 300 miles (480 kilometers) underground. One formation in Mammoth Cave looks like a frozen waterfall.

The Southeast's history also makes it a region. During the Civil War, most of the Southeastern states were part of the Confederate States of America. The first shots of the war were fired at Fort Sumter in South Carolina. At Appomattox Courthouse in Virginia, the Confederacy surrendered and ended the war.

For most of its history, the Southeast has been known as a farming region. Today new businesses have made the Southeast an industrial region. Nashville, Tennessee, is a major music center. Country music stars record many hit songs in Nashville. North Carolina leads the country in making furniture and cloth. High

The Southeast's climate creates many swampy areas.

Point, North Carolina, is called the Furniture Capital of the World. Much of the nation's living room, dining room, and bedroom furniture comes from High Point factories.

Goods from the Southeast are shipped around the world from the region's many **ports.** Louisiana has some of the busiest ports in the United States. About 70 million tons (63 million metric tons) of goods leave Louisiana each year. That's about the weight of 12 million elephants! Ships carry these goods from Louisiana to the rest of the world.

The Middle West region is a huge area of flat land with thousands of farms. Fields of green-husked corn and golden wheat cover the Middle West's twelve states. The Mississippi River cuts the Middle West almost in half. It's hard to believe that the Mississippi River begins in this region as a tiny trickle of a stream.

The Middle West is famous for its Great Lakes and the cities that have grown up along them. It is also known for its extreme weather and fierce storms. The Middle West region experiences cold, snowy winters that can lead to blizzards. Windstorms blow through in the spring and summer.

A Middle West farm

The Middle West is called the Heartland of America because it is similar to the human heart. The heart sends blood to all parts of the body to keep it alive. Farmers in the Heartland grow crops and raise animals to feed the rest of the country to keep it alive.

Farms of the Middle West region produce large amounts of milk, eggs, and grains. Because the farmers in the Middle West grow such large grain crops, the region is also known as America's Breadbasket. The country's largest crops of wheat, corn, barley, and oats are grown in the Middle West. Heartland factories process many of the farm goods into packaged foods.

21

The world's leading makers of breakfast cereals and frozen pizzas are found in the Middle West. So is the world's largest processor of beef. Packaged foods are shipped to grocery stores throughout the United States and around the rest of the world.

The flat land that is good for growing crops is also a good place for strong windstorms. In the spring and summer, windstorms called tornadoes often hit the Middle West. These storms can almost split trees into toothpicks and can pick up a house and set it down somewhere else!

Winter storms called blizzards are frequent visitors to the Middle West. A blizzard's heavy snow, strong winds, and below-freezing temperatures stop most human activities. Tall snowdrifts block city streets and highways. School can be cancelled. The blowing snow makes it almost impossible for people to see. Farmers sometimes get lost walking from their house to their barn.

Another winter storm called lake-effect snow sometimes hits land near the Great Lakes. When cold air from the Arctic blows over the warmer water of the lakes, several inches of snow can fall near the lakes.

Chicago, Illinois, sits on the shore of Lake Michigan.

At the same time, land only a few miles away from the Great Lakes might receive no snow at all.

Four of the five Great Lakes are in the Middle West. They are Lake Erie, Lake Huron, Lake Michigan, and Lake Superior. These four lakes border the two peninsulas that make up the state of Michigan. That's why Michigan is called the Great Lakes State. Through a system of canals and other waterways, the Great Lakes connect the Middle West to the Atlantic Ocean. Along this route, goods are **imported** to and **exported** from the Middle West. The Port of Duluth, Minnesota, is the country's busiest freshwater port.

The Gateway Arch of St. Louis

Another important body of water in the Middle West is the Mississippi River. Almost all the rivers that flow through the Middle West empty into the mighty Mississippi. The Mississippi starts as a small stream in Minnesota. Because the river is about 12 feet (4 meters) wide and only 18 inches (46 centimeters) deep at that point, people can take off their shoes and walk across. From there, the Mississippi flows south and forms a border of five Middle Western states. The Mississippi River then enters the Southeast region, where it finally empties into the Gulf of Mexico.

The Middle West's major cities sit along the Great Lakes and the Mississippi River system. A megalopolis stretches from Cleveland, Ohio, to Milwaukee, Wisconsin. Each city provides many things for people to see and do. Cleveland's Rock and Roll Hall of Fame and Museum presents a live radio broadcast of great rock-and-roll music. Detroit, Michigan, is known as Motor City, or Motown, because so many of the country's cars are made there. Detroit's Hitsville USA museum honors the Motown sound. Before this building was a museum, Stevie Wonder and Diana Ross recorded some of their biggest hit records there.

In 1885 the world's first **skyscraper** reached upward in Chicago, Illinois. Eight years later, the first and largest-ever Ferris wheel was built in Chicago. It held 2160 people. Today, a new Ferris wheel takes passengers up and around for a view of Lake Michigan and Chicago's many skyscrapers.

The Middle West has other sights and activities to experience. Each summer since 1973, the Annual Great Bike Ride Across Iowa takes place. This is the oldest, longest, and largest bike ride in the United States. About 15,000 bikers travel about 500 miles (805 kilometers) west to east across Iowa. They start by dipping their bike's rear tire in the Missouri River.

South Dakota's Badlands
National Park

Seven days later, the bikers dip their front tire in the Mississippi River!

The western part of the Middle West has more underground water than any other region. Because this part of the Middle West receives very little rain each year, farmers use the underground water to **irrigate** their crops.

Strange rock formations lie in an area that includes parts of North Dakota and South Dakota. Because this area is hard to travel through, it was named the Badlands. Over millions of years, wind and water formed this rocky land. Long ago, saber-toothed tigers and three-toed horses roamed across the Badlands. Today scientists find fossils of the animals that lived in the Badlands 26 million years ago.

West of South Dakota's Badlands are the Black Hills. The hills aren't really black. The dark green trees make the hills look black from a distance. Even though they're called hills, the Black Hills are mountains. One of these mountains is called Mount Rushmore. On this mountain Gutzon Borglum and hundreds of workers carved the Mount Rushmore National Memorial. In 1927 they started blasting and carving the faces of George Washington, Thomas Jefferson, Abraham Lincoln, and Theodore Roosevelt. The memorial was completed in 1941. George Washington's head is more than 60 feet (18 meters) tall!

South Dakota's Mount Rushmore

The Southwest region contains four large states: Arizona, New Mexico, Oklahoma, and Texas. This region is sometimes called the Wide Open Spaces because wide grasslands cover much of it. Herds of cattle graze on these lands. The Southwest is known for the large deposits of oil that lie under parts of it. The Southwest is also known for the history and **culture** of its Hispanic and American Indian people. The western part of the Southwest is famous for its desert and canyons.

Much of the Southwest's history is connected to Mexico. In the 1500s Spain owned Mexico. Spain also owned the land that is now in the Southwest region of the United States. Later, Spanish settlers arrived in the Southwest and built ranches. When Mexico gained its independence from Spain in 1821, it also gained control of the Southwest. Between 1845 and 1853, most of what is now the Southwest became part of the United States.

Because of the region's history, a large number of people in the Southwest today have Mexican and Spanish backgrounds. In fact, about half of New Mexico's residents are Hispanic. The Southwest is known for its hot, spicy, Mexican-style foods. Tacos, tamales, and nachos were eaten in the Southwest before they became popular throughout the rest of the United States.

The Southwest also has the largest American Indian population of any region in the United States. In the 1830s and 1840s, the United States government moved large numbers of American Indians from the Southeast to land in Oklahoma. The **descendants** of many of those people still live in Oklahoma.

Today many of the Southwest's American Indians live and work in cities. In New Mexico, however, 19 groups of American Indians live in different **pueblos.**

Cowhands at work on a ranch in the Southwest

Many of the Southwest's American Indians also honor their culture through their crafts. American Indian woven baskets, woolen blankets, pottery, and jewelry are handmade works of art.

The Southwest's wide open spaces are also sometimes known as Cowboy Country. In the late 1800s, cowboys on horseback roped cattle and herded them from Texas ranches to railroad towns in the Middle West. Today these workers are often called cowhands. They drive pickup trucks and load the cattle onto large trucks that carry the cattle to stockyards.

Cowhands ride horses and rope cattle as part of their job. They test their roping and riding skills at rodeos. These contests are held in towns throughout the Southwest. The country's first rodeo that charged admission was held in Arizona in 1888. Today the

Rodeo Hall of Fame is part of the National Cowboy Hall of Fame and Heritage Museum in Oklahoma.

One of the world's largest oil-producing areas runs through the Southwest. Texas produces about one fourth of the oil in the United States. Every county in Texas and Oklahoma has oil underneath it. Working oil wells even stand on the grounds of Oklahoma's state capitol!

Although the Southwest is wet with oil underground, dry deserts cover much of the land above ground. One of the few plants that can grow in a Southwestern desert is cactus. Cactus stems store whatever rain the desert receives. The giant saguaro cactus looks almost like a person with its thick trunk and upturned branches.

Saguaro cactus in Arizona

Farmers use underground water to irrigate the land in some Southwestern deserts. These farmers have turned desert into blooming fields of fruit and vegetables. Some of the new desert crops are watermelons, lettuce, apples, and grapes. The Gila [HEE luh] monster also lives in the desert. This poisonous lizard can go for months without eating, because it stores fat in its tail.

The Southwest contains some of the country's most beautiful sights. Big Bend National Park on the Rio Grande River forms part of the border between Texas and Mexico. After a spring rain, colorful flowers cover Big Bend. Mile after mile of red clay covers Oklahoma. White sands in part of New Mexico make up the world's largest **gypsum** desert. Some mice and lizards

Big Bend National Park

Arizona's Painted Desert

that live in this desert can turn themselves white to hide from bigger animals. Northeastern Arizona has the Petrified Forest. Trees there have turned to shiny stone over millions of years. Northwest of the forest lies the Painted Desert. At different times of the day, the rocks and sand have soft shades of brown, violet, blue, and red. The Southwest's most amazing landform is the Grand Canyon in northwestern Arizona. It is the world's largest **gorge,** measuring 1 mile (1.6 kilometers) deep, 277 miles (445 kilometers) long, and 18 miles (29 kilometers) wide at its widest point.

The West is the largest region in the United States. Eleven states, including Alaska and Hawaii, make up this region. One of its most important features is its mountains. The West contains the country's highest mountains, including the Rockies, Coastal, Cascade, Sierra Nevada, and Alaska ranges. Deserts are another feature of the West. In contrast to the deserts, **lush** rain forests grow in this region, and icy-cold glaciers slide down its mountain slopes. In fact, the West has the country's only rain forests and glaciers. Beautiful beaches line much of the West's Pacific Coast.

The Rocky Mountains

Stretching from Alaska through Colorado, the Rocky Mountains form the West's backbone. This mountain range contains most of the country's highest peaks. Pike's Peak stands at 14,110 feet (4300 meters) above sea level. It isn't the tallest mountain in the Rockies, but it's probably the best-known. Hundreds of people travel to the top of Pike's Peak every day when the weather is good. Most of them slowly drive the 30 miles (48 kilometers) of rough road to the top. On the way up, the cars hug the mountain. On the way down, drivers stay toward the middle of the road. Driving too close to the outer edge is scary and unsafe.

The Continental Divide zigzags through the Rockies. Rivers that begin on the east side of the Divide flow into the Mississippi River and empty into the Gulf of Mexico. Rivers on the west side of the Divide flow into the Pacific Ocean. At one spot in Montana, a person can stand with one foot in a river flowing east and the other foot in a river flowing west. At that same spot, a river also flows north. It is the only spot in the United States where rivers flow in three directions.

The West's mountains near the Pacific Ocean are part of the Ring of Fire, an area known for active volcanoes. This ring curves along the Pacific from South America to Alaska and on to Asia and New Zealand. Alaska has about 80 active volcanoes that could erupt at any time. In 1980 Washington's Mount St. Helens did erupt. A cloud of hot ash blew 10 miles (16 kilometers) into the sky. Sixty people died as a result of this volcano. Some towns were even buried under ash from the volcano.

Underwater volcanoes formed all the islands that make up Hawaii. Today, Hawaii's Mauna Loa is the world's largest active volcano. Nearby, Kilauea (kil oo WAY uh) has been erupting continuously since 1983.

San Francisco, California, sits on the Pacific Ocean.

As lava moves down the hill, people have to leave their homes. Some of Hawaii's beaches look like black sand. It isn't sand but finely crushed pumice (PUM ihs), which is what lava turns into once it cools.

Westerners who live in the Ring of Fire often feel earthquakes. This sudden shaking of the earth has happened many times. Many people died in the San Francisco Earthquake of 1906, and fires broke out all over the city. In 1964 Alaskans felt one of the world's strongest earthquakes. The damage cost about $750 million.

The mountains of the West are often called the nation's treasure chest. In the 1800s the biggest gold and silver rushes took place in this region. The most famous gold rush was the 1849 California Gold Rush.

People came from as far away as Ireland and China, hoping to make a fortune. The California Gold Rush boosted San Francisco's population from about 800 in 1848 to more than 25,000 in 1850. Today Nevada is the country's leading producer of gold and silver.

Rain forests are another special feature of the West. A thick rain forest grows in the Cascade Mountains of Oregon and Washington. On the sides of Mount Waialeale (wy uh LAY uh LAY) in Hawaii, rain forests receive about 460 inches (1168 centimeters) of rain each year. Waialeale is the wettest spot on Earth.

It's not surprising that rain forests grow in Hawaii's warm, wet climate. But Washington's cool, wet Olympic Peninsula also has rain forests because it receives about 140 inches (357 centimeters) of rain each year. This is North America's wettest spot.

A rain forest in Hawaii

An Alaskan glacier

Glaciers are an icy feature of the West. These huge mounds of ice slowly move down many of the region's mountains. The Malaspina Glacier covers 1500 square miles (3890 square kilometers) in Alaska, and it is North America's largest glacier. The state of Rhode Island could fit inside this glacier with room to spare.

The West is also a region of deserts. Westerners named one desert area Death Valley because so many pioneers died while crossing the area. Although few people choose to live in deserts, outlaws during the country's Wild West years used the desert for hideouts. Butch Cassidy and the Sundance Kid named their hideout in Utah Robbers' Roost. The canyons and rock formations made good hiding places. Over millions of years, wind and water shaped the rock to look like arches, bridges, and castles.

Old Faithful in Yellowstone National Park

Because the West's landscape has so many beautiful and unusual features, more than half of the country's national parks lie in this region. In 1872 Yellowstone National Park became the first national park in the world. Yellowstone is best known for its **geysers** (GY zuhrz). Yellowstone has more of these hot water spouts than any other place in the world. Steamboat Geyser, the world's tallest, shoots steamy water 380 feet (116 meters) into the air. Yellowstone's most famous geyser is Old Faithful. This geyser shoots out hot water about every 80 minutes.

The West's mighty mountains and beautiful beaches make the region an outdoor playground. Skiers speed down the West's long mountain slopes. In 1936 Sun Valley in Idaho became the country's first ski resort.

In 2002 the Winter Olympics were held in the mountains near Salt Lake City, Utah.

Surfing is a Western sport that started in Hawaii hundreds of years ago. Early Hawaiians surfed on long, heavy wooden boards. Today surfers grab their boards and head out to ride a big wave off the north shore of Oahu (oh AH hoo), one of the world's best surfing beaches. Other Western beaches draw walkers and animal lovers. Hawaii's Barking Sands Beach makes a barking sound when walkers' feet hit the dry sand. Real dogs bark at Dog Beach in California, where people and their dogs have full run of the beach. Farther north along the Pacific Ocean, sea lion pups play, and killer whales swim.

Dog Beach in Huntington Beach, California

41

Westerners also enjoy many of the region's special foods. Five kinds of salmon live in the West's northern Pacific waters. Some Westerners make their living catching or canning salmon.

The West's history also makes it a region. Many American Indians have a long history there. Pioneers who settled in the West had to travel thousands of miles. Some pioneers came in wagon trains from the Northeast and Middle West. Others sailed to the West in ships from Asia. Many settlers were strong, hardy people who built the West's mines, farms, and cities. A few were outlaws whose stories gave the region the nickname of the Wild West. By the late 1800s, the West was known as the Last Frontier. Most Americans thought the United States could go no farther than the coast. Then Hawaii entered the Union as the fiftieth state in 1959.

CHAPTER 6: FIVE REGIONS, ONE NATION

The United States contains fifty states grouped into five regions. Although they are separate states and regions, they are joined as one country. Many people in the United States come from different backgrounds, but all are known as Americans.

Americans share many of the same ideas and beliefs. They believe that everyone is equal under the law. They try to treat others fairly. They also try to respect the beliefs and thoughts of others.

Americans help each other in times of trouble, too. In 1993 the Mississippi River and other Middle West rivers flooded. The flood caused great damage to cities, towns, and farms. Americans from all over the United States helped the people of the Middle West. Some came to fill sandbags to hold the rivers back. Others sent money, clothing, and food to people who had lost their home.

Americans are proud of their country's flag.

Americans love their country and show it in many ways. Americans honor the country's one flag. Americans stand during sporting events and other activities to sing "The Star-Spangled Banner." Americans also celebrate holidays that honor important people and events in American history. On Presidents' Day, Americans honor two great Presidents, George Washington and Abraham Lincoln. On Memorial Day and Veterans Day, Americans honor soldiers who have fought for the United States. On the Fourth of July, Americans celebrate the birth of the country they love—the United States of America.

GLOSSARY

climate (KLY muht) the usual weather of a place

culture (KUHL chuhr) all the beliefs and ways of acting that belong to a group of people

descendants (dih SEN duhnts) people who come from certain other people

exported (ihk SPAWRT ihd) sent to another country to be sold there

geysers (GY zuhrz) openings in the ground through which hot water and steam shoot up into the air

glaciers (GLAY shuhrz) huge masses of slow-moving ice

gorge (gawrj) a deep, narrow valley that has steep and rocky walls, usually formed by a river running through it

granite (GRAN it) a hard, heavy type of rock

gypsum (JIP suhm) a white mineral containing calcium

harbors (HAHR buhrz) areas of water that are protected from the rougher waters of the ocean

imported (ihm PAWRT ihd) brought into a country to be sold there

industries (IN duhs treez) businesses in which goods made by machines are made and sold

inland (IN luhnd) away from the coast

irrigate (IHR uh gayt) to bring water to fields by using channels or underground pipes

limestone (LYM stohn) a kind of rock formed mainly from the shells and bones of sea animals

lush (luhsh) thick, rich, and healthy

marble (MAHR buhl) a very hard, smooth stone formed from heated limestone

megalopolis (meg uh LAH puh luhs) a long stretch of end-to-end cities and suburbs

peninsula (puh NIN suh luh) a piece of land that is surrounded on three sides by water and connected to a larger body of land

ports (pawrts) cities that have harbors where ships can load and unload goods and passengers

pueblos (PWEB lohs) American Indian villages with houses made of mud brick

regions (REE juhnz) large areas of land that are united by one or more features

skyscraper (SKY skrayp uhr) a very tall building

INDEX